Arthur Leslie Salmon

West-Country Ballads and Verses

Arthur Leslie Salmon

West-Country Ballads and Verses

ISBN/EAN: 9783744766241

Printed in Europe, USA, Canada, Australia, Japan

Cover: Foto ©Andreas Hilbeck / pixelio.de

More available books at **www.hansebooks.com**

WEST-COUNTRY BALLADS
AND VERSES

BY

ARTHUR L. SALMON

AUTHOR OF 'SONGS OF A HEART'S SURRENDER,'
ETC.

SECOND EDITION

WILLIAM BLACKWOOD AND SONS
EDINBURGH AND LONDON
MDCCCXCIX

PREFACE.

THE author owes his best thanks to Messrs Cassell for permission to republish the first portion of "Devon Lassies" from the 'Magazine of Art.' The dialect-piece "A Devon Wife" appeared in 'Longmans' Magazine'; "Autumn" in the 'Speaker'; "In the Golden Wood" in the 'Pall Mall Magazine'; and "A Song of Devon" was printed in the Summer Number of the 'Western Morning News,' 1898. With these exceptions, the contents of this little volume make their first appearance.

In the dialect-verse the author has endeavoured to reproduce faithfully the vernacular of Devonshire ; but it should be remembered that a similar dialect, with some modifications, flourishes also in part of Somerset and in East Cornwall.

CONTENTS.

PIECES IN DEVONSHIRE DIALECT.

WEST-COUNTRY BALLADS
AND VERSES.

———•———

A SONG OF DEVON.

LAND of the tor and torrent, of tillage and of
    wild,
Thou most imperial mother of many a noble child—

Thou haunt of old romances, thou nest of golden
    dreams,
Thou hope of hopeless causes, thou land of glorious
    gleams !

Give me the grace to sing thee in one exulting song,
Through whose impetuous numbers thy pulse may
    beat along,—

A

A song whose breath may echo the legends of thy
  breeze,
The magic of thy moorlands, the rapture of thy
  seas.

I see thy winding rivers in beauty seek the main,
Bringing the breath of forest, of pasture, and of
  plain ;

The kindly fostering harbours, from whence thy
  children sailed,
Who in the need of England might die yet never
  failed ;

Thy granite-heaving moorlands, whereon we dimly
  trace
Traditionary footsteps of many a vanished race :

A wilderness of heather, a paradise of gold,
Where every ancient trackway is strewn with stories
  old.

I see thy Faithful City, and many a lovely town,
Thy villages and hamlets that lurk mid furze and
  down ;

Thy gaunt and mighty headlands that front the
    Severn Sea,
Where in gigantic caverns the waves beat cease-
    lessly ;

Thy meadow-lands and orchards that blossom to the
    south ;
Thy shelving sand and shingle, thy many a river's
    mouth.

O Devon, mother Devon, whose heart is warm and
    strong,
Give me the grace to sing thee in one triumphant
    song.

Whene'er the voice of England has echoed to the
    wind,
The dauntless sons of Devon have never lagged
    behind.

They never lost their courage, they never lost their
    love :
Behind their faith in Devon lay faith in God above.

For life they lusted keenly, these playmates of the
sea ;
They never ceased to labour for England and for
thee,

Till worlds of new-born treasure poured forth their
wealth untold,
For Devon hands to gather in western lands of gold.

O Devon, mother Devon, dear country of the west,
Thine is the joy of living, thine is the peace of rest.

Thy children far may wander with hearts that toil
and yearn,
But still they hear thee calling, and still to thee
they turn.

May Devon and may England, whate'er their for-
tunes be,
In time of peace or conflict, be generous, strong,
and free !

"JAN COO."

THE air of the lonely moors for ever
　　Throbs with the pulse of the leaping river,
Where over its boulders foamingly
The Dart is fain for its haven sea.

Glorious it is when the summer gold
Is scattered widely o'er moor and wold—
When oaken leaves and ivies quiver
Responsive to the rushing river.

But when the wizard winter reigns
O'er Dartmoor wilds and Devon lanes,
With deeper tone, with keener shiver,
Dashes and dives the tameless river.

The winter sundown had ebbed and died
Over the tors and the valleys wide,
And through the hush came only the thrill
Of the moorland torrent, never still.

Brief are the toils of the winter day;
The night came fast, a phantom grey;
And round the fire the farm-folk told
Tidings and happenings, new and old.

Sudden the door flew open wide,
And the farm-boy entered, eager-eyed:
"Out in the dusk and the winter sighing
I heard the voice of a something crying."

The men rose willingly.   "Ay, for sure,
'Tis a body lost out on the moor;"
And they shouted loud where the night-time's hush
Tremulous carried the river's rush.

No cry at first.   Then clear and true
Through the air there rang, "Jan Coo, Jan Coo!"
Said they, "An' who may Jan Coo be ever?—
I'll war'n 't 'is a body down by the river."

And they shouted again, but to their crying
There came no further voice replying;
And nothing they heard and nothing they found,
Save the river's ceaseless leap and bound.

Next night again, as the shadows grew,
The same cry sounded, " Jan Coo, Jan Coo!"
And to their lusty shouts and crying
"Jan Coo, Jan Coo!" came still replying.

Then a grey-haired man said solemnly,
" For sure 'tis the pisgies [1]—that it be;
'Tis the pisgies—and whatever betide
'Tis best for us to let um bide."

Back to the fire the farm-folk went
With chilly dread and wonderment;
And they took no note of the eerie cry—
And the winter-tide dragged slowly by.

The winter slackened fast, and earth
Was quick with impulses of birth,
When through the twilight's hazy blue
The same cry came again—" Jan Coo!"

[1] Or pixies.

On the hillside stood the boy and heard,
His mind most powerfully stirred ;
And he called aloud, " I'll go and see,
Pisgy or not, what the cry may be."

Adown the slope he hotly sped
To the dips and crags of the river's bed,
While still beyond came clear and true
" Jan Coo ! "—and yet again " Jan Coo ! "

The farmer watched his headlong way,
And loudly called to him to stay ;
But the boy soon disappeared from view
Towards the cry—" Jan Coo, Jan Coo ! "

Then sudden through the nightfall chill
That lone mysterious cry was still,
And only from the gorge as ever
Trembled the pulse of the leaping river.

The night came on with dreamy gloom,
O'er tor and torrent, moss and combe ;
With deeper tone, with keener shiver,
Tumbled and tossed the tameless river.

Whether the boy might be or not
A pisgy brought to an earthly cot,
And whether from their dwellings dim
His pisgy-folk were calling him,

Or whether it was the voice of the Dart,
That every year will claim a heart—
Calling the boy to a restless grave
In the eddies of its hungering wave—

Is a question we must ask in vain.
But the boy was never seen again,
Though night and day they sought him wide
By bog and bush of the moorland-side.

And never again the moor-folk knew
That lone mysterious cry "Jan Coo!"
Where over its boulders foamingly
The Dart is fain for its haven sea.

WIDDECOMBE ON THE MOOR.

THE devil came to Widdecombe
   With thunder and with flame ;
He left behind at Widdecombe
   A terror and a name ;
And this, the moorland voices tell,
   Is how the devil came.

The autumn flashed with red and gold
   Along the Devon lanes ;
The tangled hedges of the wold
   Were rich with mellow stains,—
The torrents of the moorland old
   Were turbulent with rains.

Widdecombe on the Moor.

There came a stranger to the inn
  And sought to know his way—
To Poundstock on the moor he came
  In sombre black array;
He asked the road to Widdecombe—
  It was the Sabbath-day.

He shouted loudly for a drink—
  His sable steed he stroked ;
And when he tossed the liquor down
  It boiled and hissed and smoked;
Like water on a red-hot iron
  The hissing liquor soaked.

"Good woman, will you be my guide
  To Widdecombe on the moor?"
With trembling accent she declined—
  She said the road was sure.
She saw a cloven hoof strike out
  As he spurred away from the door.

Low on the massy cleaves and tors
  A boding trouble lay—
A ceaseless murmur of the streams
  Came through the silent day.

The stranger rode to Widdecombe,—
  Full well he found the way.

The folk were gathered in the church
  To hear the evening pray'r,
And if 'twas dark enough without,
  'Twas threefold darker there;
And on the gathered people fell
  A shudder and a scare.

Now is the time, oh kneeling folk,
  To pray with fervent fear,
For the enemy of the soul of man,
  Devouring fiend, is near,
And evil thoughts and base desires
  Unbind his fetters here.

Sudden upon the moorland kirk
  The crash of thunder broke—
A noise as of a thousand guns,
  With many a lightning-stroke,—
A blackness as of blackest night,
  With fitful fire and smoke.

It seemed the Day of doom had come;
  The roof was torn and rent,
And through the church from end to end
  A fearful flame-ball went.
It seemed the dreadful Day had come
  In wild bewilderment.

The stranger came to Widdecombe—
  He tied his horse without;
He rushed into the crashing door
  With fiendish laugh and shout;
Through the door the fiery stranger came,
  Through the shattered roof went out.

Men prayed with terror and remorse—
  In frenzied fear they cried;
And one lay dead with cloven head,
  His blood besprinkled wide—
And one was struck so dire a stroke
  That of his hurt he died.

Down through the roof the turret came—
  The spire was twisted stark.
A beam came crushing down between
  The parson and the clerk,—

And fearful was the sudden light,
  And fearful was the dark.

Then fell a deep and deathlike hush ;
  And through the silence dead,
" Good neighbours, shall we venture out ? "
  A trembling farmer said—
" I' the name o' God, shall we venture out ? "—
  For the fearsome time seemed sped.

Then up and spake the minister
  With white yet dauntless face :
" 'Tis best to make an end of prayer,
  Trusting to Christ His grace ;
For it were better to die here
  Than in another place."

So in the kirk at Widdecombe
  They finished evening pray'r ;
And then at last they ventured out
  Into the autumn air.
Brightly the jagged moorland lay
  In sundown calm and fair.

The devil came to Widdecombe
  With thunder and with flame,—
He left behind a shattered kirk,
  A terror, and a fame ;
And this, the moorland voices tell,
  Is how the devil came.

THE PARSON AND THE CLERK.

A BALLAD OF THE DEVON COAST.

WHOEVER goes to Dawlish town
　　May see, in dawn or dark,
Two rocks that front the dashing sea—
　　The Parson and the Clerk.

And till the sea hath sucked them down,
　　Which it haply soon will do,
To all the watching Devon coasts
　　They tell this legend true.

'Twas from the Faithful City
　　The parson spurred that day,
And when he came to Haldon
　　He failed to trace his way.

The storms of night were howling,
  The Wish-hounds yelled and bayed;
And the clerk, who swore he knew the track,
  Still farther from it strayed.

Their weary horses stumbled
  In ridges deep and wide,
And the parson breathed a sinful wish
  That the Fiend might be his guide.

The parson swore unholy—
  And suddenly behind
They heard a horse's clanking hoofs
  Come after like the wind.

It was a peasant mounted.
  " Good e'en to you," he cried;
" You've wandered from the trackway far,
  But I will be your guide."

With ease and skill unerring
  He led them o'er the down;
And he begged of them to sup with him
  In his house by Dawlish town.

B

" My merry friends are waiting,"
  He cried with laughter loud ;
" And to have a parson sup with them
  Will make them mighty proud."

The house looked old and crazy—
  High dashed the neighbouring sea ;
And " Thanks, my man," the parson cried—
  " We'll take pot-luck," said he.

Merry and high the feasting was,
  The guests drank deep and free ;
And the parson sang a stirring song—
  Not from the Liturgy.

A stirring song the parson sang,
  And the clerk intoned Amen ;
And when the chorus had been yelled
  They begged for it again.

And the parson shouted gladly,
  " 'Tis better than droning pray'r
In the church to the drowsy people,
  With my foxy clerk in the chair."

Loud laughed the clerk at the jesting,
  But he stooped to his master's ear,
" 'Tis best for us to be going—
  The dawn is drawing near."

" Good night, my merry masters ;
  The hour is drawing late."
And the host cried to the parson,
  " We'll see you from the gate."

The parson clomb to his saddle,
  To his dragged up the clerk ;
Strange flashes from the doorway
  Shone out into the dark.

The air was blind with sea-spray ;
  And, spite of whip and spur,
The beasts of clerk and parson
  Like rocks refused to stir.

" The Fiend is in the horses,"
  Cried the parson furiously ;
" But devil or no, we'll make them go ! "
  And the host laughed loud with glee.

Then thicker the foam descended,
　The waves more fiercely dashed,
And there stood at the door a troop of fiends
　With eyes that wildly flashed.

The crazy house had vanished—
　The breakers surged and ran ;
And to the flanks of their horses
　Clung master and clung man.

Prone on the rocks next morning
　They stretched there, stiff and stark :
On one rock lay the parson,
　On one rock lay the clerk.

Beaten and torn and mangled,
　They clung with dead-cold hands,
While their horses wandered harmless
　On shining Dawlish sands.

THE CORNISH WRECKER'S DEATH.

'TWAS the time of the barley-harvesting ;
  The wrecker lay on his bed
With the fire of grievous sin at his heart,
 Death's ice upon his head.
There came a storm-cloud from the sea,
 Thick black with fringe of red.

By his dying bed the parson stood
 With pow'rful words of pray'r.
The trembling fishers stayed without
 Nor dared to enter there,
For they heard the pirate-wrecker's groans
 And the shrieks of his despair.

There came a fearful crash and flame,
 Then deepest blackest gloom,
And it seemed as though the surging waves
 Were dashing through the room—

A fierce alternate dark and light,
　With thunderous billowing boom.

Unsteered, it seemed, by earthly hands,
　A black ship neared the shore,
Of a rig that never Cornishmen
　Had recognised before ;
And the fishers crossed themselves with dread
　As they stood around the door.

To hear the dying wrecker's cries
　Might make the bravest quail.
He yelled, "The fiend is tearing me
　With bloody tooth and nail !—
His hand is like the claw of a hawk ! "—
　And the cry became a wail.

He shouted, "Put the sailors out !—
　Their fingers drip with blood ! "—
And the shock that rent the cottage walls
　Was like the shock of a flood,
As though the breakers beat within
　With ceaseless mighty thud.

Above the wrecker's shatt'ring roof
   Hung full the cloud of night—
The deepest darkness ever known,
   While all beside was bright.
Foiled by the fiend, the parson brave
   Rushed forth into the light.

His pray'r was baffled by a heart
   Corrupt with constant sin,
Whereto no peace of penitence
   Could steal a pathway in ;
Remorse and deadly fear alone
   Can never pardon win.

Sudden the pitchy clinging cloud,
   Raised by resistless might,
Rolled from the cottage to the ship,
   And the ship began her flight.
Behind remained the wrecker's corse,
   A loathsome hideous sight.

The storm and trouble passed away
   As strangely as they fell.
There came a peace upon the earth
   As though all things were well ;

And the seaward-lying clouds became
  A field of asphodel.

Yet when they raised the wrecker's corse,
  To bury him in dread,
Rolled in the pitchy cloud again
  With fringe of lurid red,
And a sudden blaze of light caught up
  The coffin and the dead.

It whirled the coffin fearsomely
  Across the sea in flame ;
And to the outer fire he went
  Who from the darkness came ;
If there be hope for such an end,
  Such hope we dare not name.

The earth was lightened of her load—
  Sweet peace returned once more ;
The loving touch of sundown lit
  The church upon the shore.
Parson and people prayed that night
  As they never prayed before.

THE MOUTH OF THE LYN.

FORTH from the fastness of its moorland home
    With ceaseless din
Cometh the leaping Lyn,
Seeking the coast with constant fret and foam—
Bringing a wildness of the moors to wed
The wildness of the sea,—from ferny bed
And mossy boulders breaking, till it meet
The haven where its fleet
Disordered pulse shall stay its fitful beat,
And find a rest
In the more mighty swell of ocean's breast.

And when the flood-tide pours
Into the combe where Lyn first meets the sea—
When all the streamlet-shores
Are lapped in ocean's calm immensity—

There comes a silence, and the restless din
Of leaping Lyn
Is swallowed by the hush
That takes the fever from its moorland rush.
The force and turmoil of its hastening
Become a petty thing.
To listening wood and hill
Up-breathes an utter peace, and all is still.

O heart whose pulse with mad impetuous force
Frets like the moorland river,
Because the rocks and banks along its course
Impede its way for ever,—
Leave thou the self that is thy constant woe,—
Let the great flood-tide flow.
Return to thy true haven and thy source,
Merging thy wilfulness in heaven's high will.
Then shalt thou know
The heat and conflict of thy hastening
Were but a petty thing.
Hushing thy tumult and thy murmuring
Flows in the peace of God, and all is still.

SUNSET BY THE EXE.

THE flood of light falls lingeringly
　　Where Exe flows out to meet the sea,
And through my heart the flood of dream
Flows deeper with the deepening gleam.

The sun hath touched with loving hand
The stretch of sea, the bars of sand,
And on each crying sea-bird's wing
His kisses still are quivering.

The world of spirits opens wide—
The sea of soul that hath no tide;
A moment's passport comes to me,
Where Exe flows out to meet the sea.

I pass with sunset's passing gleam
Into the life that doth not dream;
The secret guarded gates unfold
Unto the self that grows not old.

In moments thus, from youth to eld,
Too briefly given, too long withheld,
The soul is snatched from time and place
To boundless peace, to boundless space.

The years that come with stain and soil,
The years of hope, the years of toil,
Pass by and leave no least impress
Upon this inmost consciousness.

Only when life of long offence
Hath dulled the soul with clouds of sense,
Rarer or none our moments be
Of glimpses at eternity;

And when the spirit's nobler need
Is sold for sordid aims or greed,
Its sleep unbroken covets not
The glories that it hath forgot.

Where Exe flows forth to meet the sea
This comfort hath been granted me :
The soul, though fast asleep it lie,
Grows never old, can never die.

ILFRACOMBE.

BY day thy ways are loud with thronging feet,
  Thy tors resound with jest and careless cries;
Thy nooks are rifled of that presence sweet
  Reserved for quiet hours and reverent eyes.
The voice of him who sells, of him who buys,
  Blend with the sea-gull's call, the wash of sea.
Thou art despoiled of beauty's modest guise,
  And loveliness hath lost her mystery.

But when the night falls and thy ways are dumb
  There comes a witching change. Upon thy shore
With fuller harmony the billows come,
  Bringing their tales of half-forgotten lore.
Our Lady of the sea is queen once more.
  Stealeth a spirit from the moorlands grey,
Taking the taint from rocky path and tor,
  Cleansing the stains that come of clamorous day.

Night hath a thousand ministers to chase
   The soilures that would mar her purity.
Lo, they have passed with no abiding trace,—
   Earth reasserts her calm supremacy :
So the polluted heart would ask to be,
   Bearing no soil of passions gone before.—
We love thee better, nursling of the sea,
   When nature claims thee for her own once more.

A LEGEND OF ST PETROCK.

ST PETROCK trod the craggy shore
    And gazed at the glowing west,
And to his heart there came a dream,
    A dream of the Isle of the Blest;—

That isle which never living foot
    With earthly stain has trod,
That lies away to the golden west,
    Somewhere in the hand of God.

There came to his feet a silver boat,
    Washed by the wave to his reach;
St Petrock stepped aboard, and left
    Sheepskin and staff on the beach.

For many days St Petrock sailed,
    Nor ate nor drank the while;
Yet he hungered not and he thirsted not
    Till he came to the Blessed Isle.

It was a land of peace and flowers,
  With valleys towards the sea—
A land of streams and singing birds,
  Where never tempests be :

Pure as the purest thoughts of heaven
  In the heart of a saint or a maid.
St Petrock left his boat by the shore,
  And trod forth unafraid.

Seven years he spent, and what he saw
  No tongue of man may say ;
But when he had spent seven years it seemed
  That he had but spent a day.

A single fruit from a tree that sprang
  Out of the verdurous sod
Was all St Petrock ate in the isle
  That lies in the hand of God.

Then he came again to the sloping beach,
  And there he found once more
The silver boat that had wafted him
  Away to this blessed shore.

Back from the Island of the Blest
    He came to the western land,
And he found his sheepskin and his staff
    Uninjured on the sand.

A grey old wolf had guarded them—
    They showed nor rent nor stain.
St Petrock stepped to the shore and donned
    His hermit-garb again.

St Petrock sailed to the Blessed Isle ;
    But when the vision broke
He found that heaven had guarded still
    His staff and sheepskin cloak.

A MOTHER'S CRY.

DO you hear the yell of the wish-hounds
   As they chase the storm to-night?
Do you hear the weary wailing—
   The cry of babes in fright?

'Tis the poor unchristen'd babies
   That the fiendish wish-hounds chase—
The souls of little babies
   That find no resting-place.

I sit by the cheerful fireside—
   I try to stop mine ear,
But the cry of the babes unchristen'd
   Sounds ever keen and near.

O God!—and in the churchyard
   My own dear baby lies—
My babe that died unchristen'd—
   Perhaps I hear his cries.

I think of the Father's mercy,
  I dream of Jesu's love ;
But the yell of the storm is near me,
  And the cry that rings above.

I cannot shut it from me,
  I cannot rest or sleep,
For my own unchristen'd baby
  Lies in the churchyard deep.

My little lamb, my darling—
  Held to the Shepherd's breast !—
But the tempest o'er the moorland
  Will give my heart no rest.

His cradle is the churchyard,
  With the Cross and Jesu's name :
On the moor the hounds are rushing
  With fangs and eyes of flame.

SEA-GULLS.

(ILFRACOMBE.)

A BOVE the misty headlands
    White sea-gulls soar and scream,
And their wings have lured the flashing
    Of the sunset's crimson gleam.
O why are those wings so restless,
    And whence that boding cry?—
Do they catch the breath of the tempest
    And the storm that is coming nigh?

Are they the souls of sleepers
    In ocean's restless bed?—
And do they speak of the living
    Or do they speak of the dead?
O why do the gulls of the ocean
    So ceaselessly circle and cry?—
Do they think of the storm that is coming,
    Or the rest that will come by-and-by?

DEVON LASSIES.

I.

FOND glances follow where she goes,
  Wooed of the wandering breeze;
The sun that 'neath her bonnet glows
  Is lured by what it sees
To write upon her blushing cheek
The words of love it fain would speak.

A cloudless gleam of summer light,
  A breath of ocean wind,
She brings a dimness to the sight
  And leaves a smile behind.
Who sees her pass will turn and bless
The God that gave such loveliness.

II.

Her eyes are like the quiet sea,
   And in their changeful deeps
I read the thought that timidly
   Within its shelter keeps.
Like sunny gleams that come and go
The ripples of her gladness flow.

The sea-bird cries above her head,
   And at her naked feet
The seaweed trembles to her tread
   And feels its pressure sweet.
The blushes of the sunset skies
Have found a refuge in her eyes.

THE CORNISHMEN AND THE CUCKOO.

THE cuckoo's is the voice of Spring,
  But Summer's ripened day
Has neared its homeward hastening
  When cuckoo flies away.

" If we could keep the cuckoo here,"
  The careful farmers sighed,
" We might have summer all the year ";
  And gallantly they tried.

They built a cunning wall around
  The cuckoo in the tree,
And circled in this narrow bound
  They said its home should be.

O cuckoo, playmate of the Spring—
  How winsome is thy call !—
The cuckoo lightly spread its wing
  And flew above the wall.

" If we had built the wall," they said,
  " Another course or so,
We know the cuckoo must have stayed ;
  We built the wall too low."

Many a season have we tried
  To make the cuckoo stay,
Yet when we thought its wings were tied
  Our cuckoo flew away.

" If we had raised the wall," we say,
  " One little inch or twain,
The cuckoo would be here to-day "—
  And then we try again.

But hands are tired of building walls
  That give a vain resistance,
And cuckoo's sweet bewitching calls
  Die sadly in life's distance.

AUTUMN.

AUTUMN came across the land,
  Tangle-haired, barefooted, brown,
And the harebells from her hand
  Quivered as she cast them down.

Eyes of deep desire and dream,
  Lips that told a haunting tale—
Cheek and brow an orchard-gleam,
  Voice, a sunset's hushing gale.

Ah, the legends that she told
  Turned the leaves to russet red—
Scattered them in showers of gold
  Over path and forest-bed.

Fern and bramble glowed with fire,
  White clematis clustered rife;
And the heart's untold desire
  Was for other fields of life.

Autumn came across the wold
  Tangle-headed, barefoot, wan ;
And her face grew sad and old—
  Darkness coming, gladness gone.

Suddenly, its madness wreaking,
  Broke a wind from out the west.
Autumn, wearied, staggering, shrieking,
  Tore her hair and beat her breast.

Woodlands groaning, sobbing, crying—
  Heaven a mass of seething cloud !—
Autumn, make an end of dying—
  Tattered leaves shall be thy shroud.

"IN THE GOLDEN WOOD."

I HELD a feasting in the golden wood
　　To which I bade old friends from far away.
　　There in the mossy covert, where the day
Wore out its hours in charmèd solitude,
I called them—ancient comrades, tried and good,
　　Dear friends of boyhood, gay when I was gay,
　　Sad in my tears and playful in my play—
I called them, waiting where alone I stood.

Alas ! no guest appeared to feast with me,
　　Save timid rabbit peeping from the fern,
And dove or wood-wren rustling in the tree
　　That overhung my stillness.　And I learn
At last, in tears, that tender memory
　　Had called them whence they never may return.

PIECES IN DEVONSHIRE DIALECT

THE PARISH CLERK.

ZO they've carried püre ol' passen tü the
    churchyard,
  An' I reckon that they oughter carry me;
For when passen says the prayers up tü glory
  'Er'll lüke for me to vollow, dawntee see?
'Twull be strange tü 'en, I warrant, güde ol' passen,
  If I shüdden help'n out wi' my Amen.
Uz be vorty year together i' the parish,
  An' tü old tü larn our reckonings agen.

They'm a-making many changes tü the church now,
  'Twid a' broken passen's 'art if 'er 'ad zeed,—
Wi' their frill-de-dills and fantysheeny trinkrums,
  What idden i' the Pray'r-Büke, as I read.
'Tis vury well for sarvice to be dacent,—
  I always 'ad'n 'spectable and vitty;
But now they'm faking up the church so fullish,
  They make'n like a play-ouze tü the city.

Our passen, zo they tell us, wuz ol'-fashioned;
    Then I reckons that I be ol'-fashioned tü.
'Er'd ride a bit tü vox-hounds of a morning,
    If zo be 'er 'ad nothen else tü dü.
They say that hunting vox beant fit for passen—
    It midden be, I dü not understan';
But 'tis a vury umman-natur'd practice,
    An' passen wuz an umman-natur'd man.

I mind how wance the Bishop come tü zee un,
    When passen 'ad a-donned 'is hunting red;
An' missis, when 'er zeed the Bishop coming,
    'Er tummilled püre ol' passen intü bed.
An' when my lard come axing for the passen,
    'Er met un vury zolemnly, tü zay,
"My 'usband be laid up wi' scarlet fayver,"—
    An' Bishop vury quickly drove away.

Ah, that wuz in his rory-tory saison,
    When 'er wuz but a vorty year or zo;
But passen 'er repented of 'is hunting—
    When 'er 'ad got tü faybul for tü go.
'Er knew zo much o' vox-hounds an' o' tarriers
    As any man tü all the countryzide;
They 'lected un tü judge mun tü the dog-show;
    But passen doffed 'is red avore he died.

Our passen düed 'is düty tü the gentry;
   'Er waited till the squire wuz in 'is sayte.
'Er praiched that all us men on airth be ekals—
   With a differns 'tween the little and the great.
I mind how wance a curate tüke the sarvice,—
   I reckon 'er wuz but a güsey thing,
For when I tell'd un "squire beant in 'is sayte yet,"
   'Er zed 'er widden wait for squire or king.

That beant the way tü taich the people düty,
   But that be how they taiches um to-day.
There wunt be any order tü the parish
   When passen an' mysel' be gone away.
I suffers zo from tissick an' brownkitty,
   It wunt be vury long avore I go:
It didden take um long tü find a passen,
   But where they'll get a clerk tü I dawnt know.

I zim the Church be gwain tü get a tummil—
   'Tis Pappistry, zo far as I can zee;
An' Pappistry be wurse than Nonconformies,
   Accordin' tü ol' passen an' tü me.
I darezay that uz be a bit ol'-fashioned,—
   The Bible it must be ol'-fashioned tü.
I'd rayther vollow vox-hounds wi' the passen
   Than listen tü their fullish fillyloo.

It beant for want of charutty an' kindness,—
　　Our passen wuz zo kind's a man can be ;
Uz jogged along wi' Methody and Baptiss,
　　Zo long's they didden interfere wi' we.
Uz kep the Christen customs right and proper,
　　But I warrant now the divel 'ull come home.
There's a proper place for everything, zed passen,
　　An' the proper place of Romans is tü Rome.

Yü shüde 'a heard the singing and the hanthems
　　Uz giv'um tü the church o' Sabbath-days ;
With clarinet and viddle and with 'cheller,
　　Uz taught'n how tü sing an 'ymn o' praise.
But passen 'er got doiled and tüke an organ—
　　Zims totally unscripterral tü me ;
There beant a word o' organs where the Scripter
　　Zes "zackbut, vlüte, and 'arp an' psalterie."

An' zo I've zeed the end o' püre ol' passen ;
　　'Er tottled, last I zaw'm, upon 'is legs.
I reckerlecks a varmer tü a dinner,
　　As prayed for fewer passens and more pegs.
'Tis trüe that pegs be vury handy crayters,
　　An' üsefuller than passens when they'm dead—
But yü might zay the same o' clerks, I reckon,
　　An' sartainly I widden 'ave it zed.

It idden that I undervally pegs now,—
   I widden be zo thankless tü the Lard;
But zomehow clerks an' passens goes together,—
   An' passen he be gone tü his reward.
An' when 'er gets tü praying, up tü glory,
   'Er'll lüke tü me tü vollow up 'is pray'r;
When Scripter müvèd 'im in zundry plazes
   I wuz always purty sartain tü be there.

A DEVON WIFE.

WHATIVER dü 'er kep on vor? 'Er niver
be 'appy, 'er baint,
Unless 'er can bullyrag zomebody ; an' I be zo meek
as a zaint !
I've always a-bin a gude 'usband, a proper gude
'usband to she,
But 'er be a rampaging, drabitted, fussocky body,
'er be.

I can't a-zay 'er be lazy, vor that baint azackly trüe ;
Yü niver did zee anybody rout about 'ouze as 'er
dü ;
But Zolomon 'as zed, an' I reckon et's trüe as my
life—
Better an 'ouze unvitty than a clapper-clawing wife.

What wi' 'er crinkum-crankums, dang my ole wig
    vor me,
Ef 'er idden a wapsy wife as iver a man could zee !
'Er 'oppeth about the 'ouze like a cat upon 'ot
    bricks,
Wi' niver an end to 'er crāking an' fanty-sheeny
    tricks.

When vurst I come to know 'er, 'er wur zo mild as
    milk—
A müty-hearted maiden wi' skin zo soft as silk ;
But loramassy ! now 'er's quite a different crayter,
Wi' tongue foriver clappin', an' skin zo rough as a
    grater.

But yet 'er be my missis, the chillern's mawther
    too ;
'Er's wan of the right zort, 'er is, at bottom, that be
    true ;
An' what I 'ave zed, I'll zay et—I'll stand by what I
    'ave zed—
But ef any one else should zay et, I'll vetch'n a
    clout'n tha head.

Düee think I don't remember that Satterday in
    Jüne ?—
Us stüde in the daffadowndillies, us lüked up at the
    müne ;
Us hadn't a deal to zay, but I'll warrant us thought
    the moar,
An' a purtier little maid there niver was zeen avore.

Us lüked up at the müne as ef us niver had zeed 'er,
An' then I lüked in 'er eyes as though my lüke cud
    read 'er.
Zed I, " Et's a bütiful night "; 'er answered an' zed,
    " Zo et is ";
An' zomehow I seed no rayson why I shudden
    make vor a kiss.

Fegs ! I wuz only a bwoy; an' I zed, " There is
    pisgies here ;"
I knew 'er wuz feared o' pisgies, an I drü a bit
    more near.
I tellee I niver feared the pisgies in the laist,
But I thort et a gude excüse to vetch my arm roun'
    'er waist.

I didn't zee 'er then a rampaging, drabitted zoul—
'Er wuz a purty maid, wi' eyes zo black as a coal;
'Er wuz a purty maid, an' I wuz only a bwoy,
An' I liked 'er all the moar that 'er was a trifle coy.

An' zomehow et come about, what wi' the pisgies
    an' müne,
I axed 'er tü be my missis, et couldn't be too züne.
I dunno what 'er answered—et wasn't No 'er zed—
An' as 'er lived tü Kirton,[1] tü Kirton us wuz wed.

'Er beant the zame azackly as 'er appeared that day;
It beant no gude to argyfy, 'er's bound tü get 'er way.
I've always bin a gude 'usband, a rare gude 'usband
    to she,
An' 'er's bin gude at the vittles, whativer 'er temper be.

A rare un at the vittles, an' everything be nayte;
'Er knows to manage vitty tha tatties an' the mayte.
A little short tü temper—I'll stand tü what I've
    zed—
But ef any one else should zay et, I'll vetch'n a
    clout'n tha head.

[1] Crediton.

I beant a bwoy no longer, tü be takken wi' a show ;
I wants a busy missis tü make the vittles go.
Let 'er be vretful zometimes, and clapper-claw a
    gude un—
In a' the countryzide there beant 'er equal at 'ogs-
    pudden.

A purty vace wur zummut, but when I marriet, züne
I vound there's zomething else to dü than lüking at
    tha müne ;
An' when the chillern come to us tha coortin' days
    wuz done—
There's zummut more to thenk of now than ninny-
    hammer vun.

Whativer dü 'er kep on vor ?   But if et pleases she,
I can't azackly reckon that it does much hurt to me ;
An' if the Almighty tüke 'er, as wuz a purty maid,
I warrant I'd want to vollow an' lie whur she be laid.

"VIDDLE-DEE."

I TOLD 'er 'twuz tha pisgies, but 'er answered
  " Viddle-dee !"
'Er zed that I wuz tosticated tü.
'Er's zackly like a haythen an' an infidul, 'er be,
  A-doubtin' an' a-scornin' what be trüe ;
    An' 'ow can I reply
    When 'er zes " Tes all my eye,"—
  When 'er's yalling like a yaffer an' zes " Boo "?

'Twuz coming from tha market, as I got upon tha
  müre,—
  I 'adn't turned my westkit inzide-out,—
An' there bezide tha fuzzes wuz tha pisgies, tü be
  shüre,
  Tha pisgies that my mawther told me 'bout ;
    When I wuz but a kid
    'Er wid tell o' mun, 'er wid—
  An' mawther knew a thing or tü, naw doubt.

Tha müne wuz zhinin' bütivul, but I'd a-lost my
    way—
  I've bin along an 'underd times avore.
The pisgie-volk they played wi' me an' laided me
    aztray,
  Till I wandered an' I blundered more an' more.
    Then I thinks, "Yer zilly lout!
    Turn yer westkit inzide-out,"—
  An' I quickly turns ma westkit backsivore.

Et wuzn't very welcoming, when I got hum that
    night,
  Vor tha missis tü be zaying "Viddle-dee."
I might a' bin a-drownded i' tha goyals out o' zight,
  An' what wid 'er a' done withouten me?
    'Er lüked me 'ead tü füte,
    An' 'er zed, "Yer drunken brüte!"
  An' the pisgies, zo 'er zed, wuz viddle-dee.

'Er tummilled me tü bed in such a hugger-mugger
    way,
  When I waked I vound me bütes upon me fayte.
'Er's bin tü crooked words wi' me an' glumpin' all
    tha day,

Because that I wuz pisgie-led an' layte.
   Whativer I zes tü she
   'Er answers " Viddle-dee."
I'm crüel dissappointed wi' 'er prate.

Ef this be eddication, then it's zinful, zo I zay—
   A taichin' disrespeck o' what is trüe.
When vather met tha pisgies i' tha güde ol'-vash-
      ioned way,
   Ma mawther 'er believed 'im drü-an-drü.
      'Er niver wid a' zed,
      " You'm a-tosticated, Ted "—
Vor 'er trusted in ma vather, an' 'er knew.

When next I goes tü market wi' tha bastes an'
      garden stuff,
   Ma missis be a-comin' by ma zide ;
An' ef 'er zee tha pisgies 'er'll believe me shüre
      enough,
   An' ef 'er dawnt 'er'll reckon that I lied.
      But dallee ! I mid swear,
      Ef tha pisgies shüde be there,
They'll zee ma missis comin' an' they'll hide.

A DEVON SWAIN.

DAWNT spake tü me like that again, I tellee,
    for I dü veel quare,—
My mind is kind of in a maze, an' I might jit 'ee
    unaware ;
'Zides which, I beant a-gwaine tü zee that zilly smile
    upon thee face,
An' ef thee dissent mend thee ways I'll dap 'ee in a
    tender place.

"I'es love, I tellee—love, for sure ; an' love is what
    thee dissent knaw—
A vire within me buzzum 'ot, wi' bellises at constant
    blaw,—
One bellis blawed by Kitty Combe, an' one be
    blawed by Zarey Ann,
An' one by Molly Mux'orthy,—my fey ! I be a lov-
    ing man !

I'll tellee ef thee listens kind, but not ef thee be
  pokin' game ;
'Tes gude tü 'lleviate tha mind o' zum o' ets tur-
  menting vlame.
Thee knaws I always wuz a zoft and müty-hearted
  zort o' chap,
An' vury tender tü tha girls,—naw, ef thee grins I'll
  gie 'ee a dap.

When I wuz but a dawy bwoy I loved a dizzen maids
  or moar,
But that wuz just a babby's play, an' naw I love
  about a score.
But 'taint azackly quantity that makes my heart zo
  'ot's a vlame—
'Tes qualutty, I tellee, lad—tha qualutty beant naw
  tha zame.

For what's tha veelings of a bwoy compared tü veelings of a man ?
An' what wuz all they güsey maids compared to Moll
  an' Zarey Ann,
Or Kitty Combe or Betty Butt, an' all they other
  purty things,
That makes me love um all tu-wance, and wish I 'ad
  a dizzen wings ?

They zay 'tes bad tü have tu minds, an' tü be pulled
    tu ways tu-wance ;

I'm passelled quite a score o' ways an' led an igsy-
    pigsy dance.

My 'art be in a power o' bits—a differnt bit, a differnt
    girl—

An' when I tries tü thenk et out I gets complately
    in a twirl.

I've lost my d'raxions totally—I'm burned ef I dü
    knaw my way—

An' then zome other chap comes round like Dicky
    Pearse tha t'other day,—

For just as I wuz 'bout tü ax Maria Rook tü be
    my wife,

That Dicky come an' married 'er, my awn Maria,
    'pon my life !

An' Kitty Combe, my bütivul ! they tells me 'er's
    engaged to Jack,

An' Loramassy ! I dü veel that I shüde be upon
    'es track ;

But then ef 'er shüde diddle Jack an' come along
    tü yümmer me,

There's purty 'Liza Widecombe—'ow could I dü
    withouten she ?

An' then there's Susie Toller tü—I always vound
   'er vury civil ;
Er's nayte an' yet not gaudy, as they zed tü ol' time
   o' tha divel ;
They painted un a bright pay-green, and tied 'es tail
   with ribbings red,
An' " Nayte, not gaudy," as I yer, is just azackly
   what they zed.

'Tes turrabul tü be distract in sich a manner as I
   be,
An' ef I ax the volk's advice, they snigger 'stead
   o' symperthy.
Tha zilly chuckle-headed vules ! they awnly thenk
   tü zwill and ayte ;
But love be moar than appetite, an' love be moar
   than drink or mayte.

I'm like a moth be in tha light,—but didee iver
   veel tha pain ?—
I reckon that thee niver did—thee niver loved wi'
   might an' main.
Thee may 'av loved a zingle maid, perhaps—naw,
   dawntee luke zo 'skance—
Thee niver loved a dizzen maids, an' loved the
   dizzen all tu-wance.

Na, I be zartin that thee ant; a zingle maid's
    enough for thee.
I wants tü marry 'arf a score, and that, they zay,
    be pollig'my.
But pollig'my or biggimy beant vitty for a Christen
    land;
I thenk I'll try tü make a choice an' put tha matter
    out o' hand.

An' what düee thenk o' Zarey Ann?—'er be a purty
    piece o' gudes;
But then there's Katey Culliford, and jimminy!
    there's Polly Woods—
An' Jenny Gribble, an' tha lot,—aw my, et's comin'
    on again!—
My buzzum's like a hotted awn,[1] an' thee be snig-
    gerin' at my pain.

Naw, ef thee dissent mend thee ways I'll dap 'ee
    in a tender place,—
I beant a-gwaine tü zee thee grin zo dashus in my
    vury vace.

[1] Oven.

Thee didden mean et, düee zay? Aw well, then,
    I'll vorgive 'ee, lad—
But dawntee dü et any moar; I tellee straight, I
    dü veel bad.

Let's 'ave a mug o' zider, bwoy, an' drink tü all they
    girls o' mine;
An' ef thee 'as a vancy tü, we'll alzo drink a mug tü
    thine.
We'll take thee maiden zepparate, but mine we'll
    zwaller i' tha lump,—
I cudden give a drink tü aich, excep' wi' watter
    from tha pump.

My eyemers! I be 'ungry tü—I reckon love's an
    'ungry thing;
Wi' all they bellises at work, my vurnace be just
    galloping;
An' ef thee thinks I ayte a deal, just reckerleck
    this zarcumstance:
Et takes a deal tü veed a man what loves a score o'
    girls tu-wance.

IN THE DIMPSES.

I LOVE tü zit i' the dimpses,[1]
  When the night begins tü vall,
An' zee the dear ol' vaces
  An' yer the voices call.
In daytime I be lonezome—
  The volks kep far away;
But they come tü me i' the dimpses,
  At the end o' the long long day.

I don't a-mean the chillern,
  Though they be güde, I know,
But I dü mean the missis,
  Whü died a year ago,—
An' I dü mean my mawther—
  'Er's long bin gone away;
They come to me i' the dimpses,
  Though they midden come tü stay.

[1] Twilight.

I zit i' the chimbly cornder
  An' watch the virelight dance,
An' fill my ol' churchwardin,—
  The missis filled it wance.
It almost zimmeth zometimes
  'Er lights my pipe agen ;
An' I smokes my ol' churchwardin
  As I üsed to smoke'n then.

I beant zo chuckle-headed
  As yü may think I be,
But the wits of my ol' missis
  Wuz enough for 'er and me ;
An' now 'er beant a-nigh me
  I'm awkard-like, no doubt,—
But I beant zo doiled i' the dimpses,
  When I thinks 'er be about.

If yü come to me i' the dimpses
  To tell o' craps an' weather,
Yü'll think I've bin a-draming
  An' my wits beant pulled together.
I'll ax 'ee tü excüse it
  That I should treat 'ee zo ;
I wuz talking wi' the missis
  As died a bit ago.

A DISTRICT VISITOR.

'TES kind of 'ee tü come and lave yer tracks tü
    tha door,
But all tha same, I'll ax 'ee not dü et any moar.

I beant a forrin haythen, nur yet be I a saint,
Nor yet be I a pauper; I dawnt mak no complaint.

When things be right and vitty, I goes tü church
    an' prays;
Accordin' tü my knawledge I lüke tü men' my ways.

Accordin' tü my knawledge,—'tes much as wan can
    dü;
Tha Lard wunt ax no moar o' me nor yet o' yü.

But what then dü 'ee offer ef I read them tracks
    tü-day?—
Be it tha loan o' a blanket, or 'arf a pun' o' tay?

An' ef I comes tü yer maytings vor tha benefit o'
    my soul,
Of course yü'll gie me a ticket vor 'arf an underd
    o' coal?

Aw 'ess ! There's Sally Skedger ain't 'tickular wher
    'er goes
So long as et brings a passel o' vittels an' winter
    clothes.

Yü bids vor tha biggest nummer, an' course yü 'as
    tü pay ;
Ther's a power o' competition vor tha savin' o' souls
    tü-day.

A power o' competition, an' yü heads tha list, na
    doubt,—
But dawnt yü think that tha Lard may be strikin'
    a few names out?

And dawntee think, ma cheel, 'twid be better tü
    stay away
Than tü go tü wuship awnly vor tha sake o' a pun'
    o' tay?

Church or chapel or both, I reckon et's just tha
    same :
A thing ain't any tha better 'cause two can play at
    tha game.

But ef et's a matter o' barter, I warrant a body's
    soul
Ain't tü be bought wi' a ticket vor 'arf an underd o'
    coal.

You'm like tha 'totallers tü,—they argifies just tha
    same ;
Ef a body 'll tak tha pledge they thinks un tha crap
    o' tha crame.

They'm right tü be down on tha drink, but ther's
    many I knaws tü-day
Pledges a dizzen times vor tha sake o' tha buns an'
    tay.

Ther's some tü 'onest tü promise moar'n they thinks
    they'll du ;
Ther's some as 'll promise ought, an' niver a word
    o' et trüe.

'Tes kind 'o yü tü come and lave yer tracks tü tha
    door,
But I dawnt fin' time tü read um,—I guess I've
    told 'ee avore.

Ther's wan gude lady come i' tha marnin', t'other
    day,
When I wuz tearin' wi' work, an' wanted tü zit an'
    pray.

Tha 'ouse wuz all in a jakes, an' tha vittels 'ad all tü
    be cüked ;
When tha vokes cam 'ome tü dinner a purty drab
    I'd a-lüked.

Sed I, " I'll ax 'ee tü 'scuse et ; I beant in a vitty
    state.
Tha vokes 'll be comin' süne, an' ther's nothin' vor
    mun tü ayte ;

An' tha chimmers must all be clayn'd, an' I can't
    fin' time, no fay !
But ef yü come i' tha dimmets, you'm welcome tü
    zit an' tü pray."

'Er give me an anger'd lüke, an' "Wumman," 'er
    stiffly sed,
" Yü prizes tha food o' airth more than tha Living
    Bread."

Then up I got an' spake.   " Tha Lard 'ath gi'en us
    mayte,
An' 'tes a wumman's duty tü mak'n vit tü ayte.

" I 'aves my duty tü 'ome,—et mid be tha same wi'
    thee ;
But dawnt be comin' yer wi' texes an' tracks tü
    me."

I knaw I wuz wrong tü spake in sich a wapsy
    way,
But I thort that tha wumman 'ad sed what 'er 'adn't
    no right tü say.

'Er niver 'll come agen—I can't say I'm sorry o'
    that ;
But yü be so welcome as Spring tü come i' tha
    dimmets an' chat.

But dawnt be bringin' yer tracks. I knaw you'm a
  proper zort,
Though yü belongs tü tha chapel an' I be church
  up-brort.

I'll niver begurge tü listen after tha work o' tha
  day,—
But marnin's, my dear sawl! ther beant no time tü
  pray.

THE CURATE.

PASSEN 'ad a bran'-nü cureit
    Mannyfacter'd tü tha town;
'E wuz licensed by tha Bisshop
    Tü wear rid upon 'es gown.

Passen's beard be long and vuzzy,
    Jist a maze o' tuzzled 'air;
Cureit's tattie-trap an' muzzle,
    Like a bwoy's, be smooth an' bare.

Passen be o' rid complaxion,
    Varmer-like an' gert an' strong;
Cureit lüketh pale and pittice,
    An' 'es vace be thin an' long.

Passen pracheth straight an' manly,
    Like er spaketh tü our vace;
Cureit pracheth vine an' screechy,
    Wi' a deal o' airs an' grace.

All tha maids wuz mad on cureit—
    Thoat'n sich a purty thing—
Quite a tiddivated angel,
    Special brand for wushipping.

Cureit lüked upon tha maidens
    An' tha widders, ca'm an' zwate,—
Volded 'ands an' zed zo zaintlike,
    "Vrends, I be a sellybate."

"Sellybate! An' what be that now?"
    All tha zilly güses ax,
An' they rinned, zo mad as 'atters,
    Tü ther bükes o' words an' vacks.

Drü tha printed bükes they rampaged—
    Little cüde they understan';
An' they zes, tha wan tü t'other,
    "Sellybate be zingle man."

"Cureit tells us 'e be zingle—
    Course 'er be, tha purty dear!—
What 'er manes es that 'er's waiting
    Till tha proper maid appear."

Ivery maiden lüked 'er naytest,
  Like a hadge o' vlowers in May ;
Ivery widder lüked 'er slyest,
  Thrawin' shape's-eyes in 'es way.

Then tha cureit prached a zarmun,
  An' wuz careful tü egsplain
"Sellybate manes vargin-zingle ;—
  Zo I be, an' zo remain."

All tha maidens an' tha widders
  Tossed ther 'eads, zo mad's mid be,
An' they zed tha cureit's zarmun
  Wuz tha plainest pappistry.

"'Er be doiled an 'er be dotty,"—
  An' a power o' other things ;
"Zilly, dawy, beardless napper !"—
  Cureit 'ath a-doffed 'es wings.

A DEVON SCHOOLMASTER.

'TIS written in tha güde ol' Büke, "There's
nothing nü beneath tha sun ";
An't ain't for me to conterdick tha cunning words
o' Zolomon.
But if yü axes me my mind, I think 'twould be
more trüly told,
Not zackly that there's nothing nü, but that they'm
leaving nothing old.

They'm leaving nothing old, excep a fü ol' men the
like o' me,
And us be feeling out o' place in a' this jimcrack
company.
Us be forgot and unbeknawn; ther's nothing left
for us to dü
But get away tü Kingdom come, and let um make
tha world anü.

They think us proper natterals ; it midden be polite
    to say
In raisonable language what us sometimes comes to
    think of they.
Tha maidens and the nappers what I eddicated tü
    tha sküle,
They think their ol' skülemaister now na better than
    a knaw-nort füle.

They've got a gert nü Boord-sküle now, an' taich a
    mighty lot o' truck,
Wi' algybries and chimistries tü babbies hardly left
    tü suck.
They gives a deal o' sküling there—they chuck'm
    full o' facks, na doubt,
But eddication is a thing they dawnt a-zim tü know
    about.

There's many a napper shüde a' helped his father tü
    tha farming-work,
As thinks 'eeself tü güde for that, and must be what
    they calls a clerk ;
But what the güde o' sküling is I nivver could pre-
    tend tü see,
Unless it fits a bwoy to fill the corner where his
    duty be.

An' for tha maids, they taiches um tha mattymatics
    an' pianner—
I reckon vittels beant a-cüked no longer in the güde
    ol' manner ;
Tha ninny-hammer güses now just turn wi' mimpsy-
    pimsy scorn
An' proudness from tha wholesome lives their püre
    ol' mawthers lived avore'n.

Avore they had tha Boord-sküle built, when I wuz
    maister tü tha sküle,
I taiched um how to read an' write, and 'rithmetic
    by simple rüle ;
No jomettries and algybries—I taiched according
    tü my light,
Tü worship God and shame tha dowl, tü spake tha
    truth and dü tha right.

They didden larn for ornament—they larned for use
    and daily toil ;
They larned that hands be made for work and feet
    must sometimes take a soil.
Tü train tha 'art is güder far than simply eddicate
    tha mind ;
I've nort against tha Sküle-boord if it makes tha
    chillern güde an' kind.

There wuz a terrubul storm one day—the sea wuz
    shouting tü tha land ;
An' on tha shore, a six mile off, they found a bwoy
    upon tha sand—
A little bwoy tha sea had dashed an' brought tü
    shore an' laid un there,—
A little bwoy—his mawther wance had kissed an'
    folded back his hair.

Down on tha coast, six mile away, they'm used tü
    wrecks an' death, they be ;
But hearing o' this little lad, I'll own it quite come
    over me ;
An' when tha passen buried un, I tüke tha chillern
    tu an' tu
Tü follow sorrowful behind tha little bwoy whom no
    one knew.

Tü talk about that little bwoy was better for tha
    chillern far
Than all their chimistries and truck, and all their
    'zamminations are ;
For àll tha nappers an' tha maids—ay, an' tha grey
    ol' maister tü—
Wuz none ashamed tü cry about tha little bwoy
    whom no one knew.

God bless tha little bwoys an' maids ! I wuz a father
 tü um all ;

I often sits an' thinks o' mun, what time tha dimpsy-
 shadows fall ;

I beant a married man, yü see, and now that I be
 old an' grey

I miss tha rowstering bwoys an' girls—I miss um
 more than I can say.

I often sits an' thinks o' mun. Tü me they'm always
 girls an' bwoys,

Wi' cheeks so red as quarrenders, an' purty lükes
 an' merry noise.

They'm all grown men an' women now, and some be
 gone across tha sea,

An' some be in their churchyard-beds ; they'm
 always bwoys an' girls tü me.

They tell me if I tried tü pass tha 'zamminations tü
 tha süle

I'd just be in tha hinfants' class an' sit upon tha
 dunce's stüle.

Ah, well, I nivver did profess such power o' intel-
 lecks as some,

An' jommettries wunt be no use when I be gone tü
 Kingdom come.

www.ingramcontent.com/pod-product-compliance
Lightning Source LLC
Chambersburg PA
CBHW032351020726
47499CB00008B/2702